Autumn's Emergency

Autumn's Emergency

By

David M. Sargent Jr.

Illustrated by

Jean Lirley Huff

Ozark Publishing, Inc.
P.O. Box 228
Prairie Grove, AR 72753

Library of Congress Cataloging-in-Publication Data

Sargent, David M., 1966-
  Autumn's emergency /c by David M. Sargent Jr. ; illustrated by Jean
Lirley Huff.
      p. cm.
Summary: Autumn comes to the farm and guards it faithfully.
  ISBN 1-56763-565-2 -- ISBN 1-56763-566-0 (pbk.)
  [1. Dogs--Fiction. 2. Stories in rhyme.] I. Huff, Jean Lirley, 1946-
ill. II. Title.
  PZ8.3.S2355 Au 2000
  [E]--dc21
                                    00-012095

Inspired by

Autumn and all the trouble she finds, whether looking for it or not.

Dedicated to

Autumn. You're just a big ole goof ball.

Vera, Mary, and Buffy made a new friend around town.
Her name is Autumn and she's big and brown.

She came to live with us on the farm.
She's really sweet and does no harm.

I gave her a job and she does it well.
She guards the farm over hill and dell.

She chases the rabbits, squirrels, and coons,
Then plays with them all day like a big ole goon.

She never eats them or hurts them in any way.
She just wants to make them play the day away.

At night, she gets to sleep in the house.
Although she's big, she's as quiet as a mouse.

One morning early I let her out.
The farm, you see, needed its scout.

On this day when she came home,
She was tattered and torn and cut to the bone.

Her body looked bad but I could see in her eyes,
It was not yet time to say the goodbyes.

We raced to the doctor's to get some help.
She never cried once, nope, not a yelp.

The doctor gave stitches while I sat and prayed
And remembered all the times Autie and I have played.

About three weeks later she was as good as new
And eager to go home because she had a job to do.

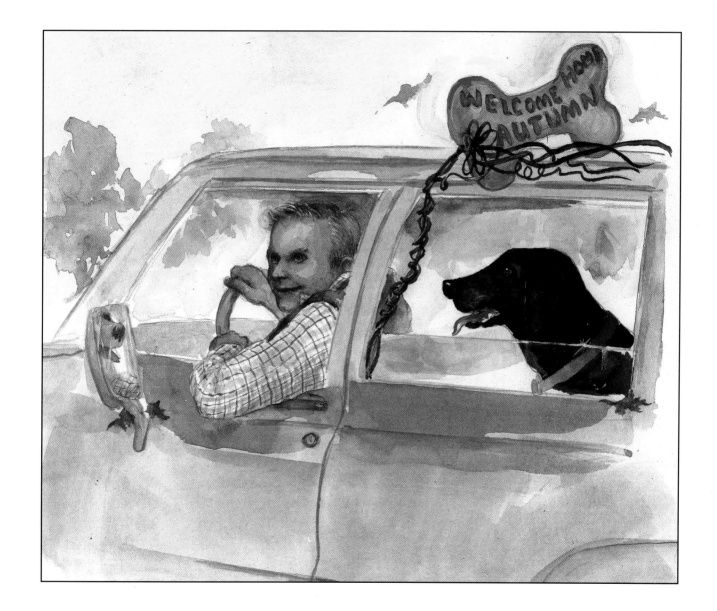

She still guards the farm both night and day.
But now she never wanders very far away.